Months of the Year

With Macy

Written and Illustrate By:
Christine Kuschewski

"Mom, I want to learn about the months of the year. Do you think you can teach me?" asked Macy.
"I would love to teach you!" replied her mom.

January

January is the first month of the year. There are 31 days in January. The 1st day of January is New Year's Day. This is when we celebrate the start of the new year.

January

Macy's birthday is January 9th! She loves to celebrate her special day.

February

The second month of the year is February. February is the only month with 28 days. Every 4 years there are 29 days in February. When this happens, it is called a leap year. Love is celebrated on Valentine's Day. Valentine's Day is February 14th.

March

March is month number three! March has 31 days. The 17th of March is St. Patrick's Day. We wear green for good luck on this day and celebrate Irish heritage.

MARCH 2022

SUN	MON	TUE	WED	THU	FRI	SAT
		1	2	3	4	5
6	7	8	9	10	11	12
13	14	15	16	17	18	19
20	21	22	23	24	25	26
27	28	29	30	31		

April

April is the fourth month of the year. April has 30 days, and we celebrate Easter. The day is different each year.

May

May is month number five. There are 31 days in May. We celebrate our mothers on the second Sunday of May each year.

MAY 2022

SUN	MON	TUE	WED	THU	FRI	SAT
1	2	3	4	5	6	7
8	9	10	11	12	13	14
15	16	17	18	19	20	21
22	23	24	25	26	27	28
29	30	31				

June

June is the sixth month of the year. June has 30 days. We celebrate our fathers on the third Sunday of June each year.

July

The seventh month is July. There are 31 days in July. On the 4th day we celebrate America's independence. There are parades and fireworks on the Fourth of July.

August

The eighth month is August. August has 31 days. There are no major holidays celebrated in August, but it is viewed as the end of summer since many children return to school in August.

September

September is month number nine. There are 30 days in September. Labor day is celebrated on the first Monday of the month. September is also the month when we harvest apples.

SEPTEMBER 2022

SUN	MON	TUE	WED	THU	FRI	SAT
				1	2	3
4	5	6	7	8	9	10
11	12	13	14	15	16	17
18	19	20	21	22	23	24
25	26	27	28	29	30	

October

The tenth month of the year is October. There are 31 days in October, and Halloween is celebrated on the 31st. On Halloween children dress up in costumes and go to houses in their neighborhood to trick or treat.

OCTOBER 2022						
SUN	MON	TUE	WED	THU	FRI	SAT
						1
2	3	4	5	6	7	8
9	10	11	12	13	14	15
16	17	18	19	20	21	22
23	24	25	26	27	28	29
30	31					

Priority _____ _____ _____

November

November is the eleventh month of the year. There are 30 days in November. Thanksgiving is celebrated on the fourth Thursday of the month each year. Families celebrate with feasts just like the pilgrims and native Americans did years ago.

NOVEMBER 2022

December

The twelfth and last month of the year is December. December has 31 days. We celebrate Christmas on the 25th day each year. Children love Santa Claus.

"Wow! That is a lot to remember, mom," said Macy.

"You are right, Macy. However, just remember there are 12 months and each month has a major holiday with the exception of August. You can sing a song to help you remember the order, " replied mom.

"But how will I remember how many days are in each month?" asked Macy. "That's easy. There is a little rhyme that will help. Thirty days has September, April, June, and November, all the rest have thirty-one, except February at twenty-eight, but leap year, coming once in four, February then has one day more." mom told Macy.

"That's great!" exclaimed Macy.

Macy thanked her mom for teaching her all about the months of the year, but now she wanted to know about the days of the week.
"Let's work on that tomorrow, Macy," replied her mom.

Macy's World Titles

Christine Kuschewski has been a special education teacher for 22 years. She loves teaching children how to read. Her love for books and education has led her to writing children's books. Christine and Macy live in Arizona. Macy loves to spend time with her best friends, Toby, Kona and their family. Macy is a 7 year-old Bichon Frise, Poodle, Maltese and Shih-Tzu mix. Everyone who meets Macy falls in love with her. Together Christine and Macy enjoy spreading love to the world.

Love Queen
LET YOUR LOVE SHINE THROUGH

15815930R00022